LEGEND OF THE BLACK JEWEL

Hunter Family Missionary Series

Book 3

Mike Bell

Beacon Hill Press of Kansas City
Kansas City, Missouri

Copyright 1999
by Beacon Hill Press of Kansas City

Printed in the United States of America

ISBN 083-411-7606

Cover Design: Keith Alexander
Illustrator: Dave Howard

Editor: Bruce Nuffer
Editorial Assistants: Andrew J. Lauer and Alicia Hilton

Unless otherwise indicated, all Scripture quotations are taken from the *Holy Bible, New International Version®* (NIV®). Copyright © 1973, 1978, 1984 by International Bible Society. Used by permission of Zondervan Publishing House. All rights reserved.

Note: This book is part of the Understanding Christian Mission, Children's Mission Education curriculum. It is designed for use in Year 4, The Missionary. This study year examines how missionaries live and how their work impacts the lives of others. This book emphasizes the variety of jobs God calls missionaries to do. The characters and stories in this story are fictional.

10   9   8   7   6   5   4   3   2   1

Contents

1. The Legend — 5
2. The Trap — 11
3. Black Jewel of the Sun — 18
4. Tested Faith — 22
5. In Nairobi — 26
6. Nowhere to Run — 31
7. The Black Castle — 35
8. He's Back — 40
9. Inside — 45
10. Crossed Signals — 49
11. The Explanation — 54
12. Shattered — 58
13. Rescued — 63
14. The Legend Dies — 68

1

The Legend

The roar from the large engines drowned out the explosions dotting the field next to the Sudan airstrip. But Robert Simpson could still hear his heart pounding wildly in his ears. He raced to throw supplies onto the plane.

"Leave the supplies, Robert, and jump on." Matuma, Robert's assistant, yelled to him from the open doorway of the cargo plane.

The plane began to move slowly as Robert jogged along the side. Wind from the powerful engines picked up dirt and grass and threw it into his face. A bomb exploded nearby, then another. They were getting closer.

Robert wanted to scream, *"We're missionaries! We're here to help!"* However, he knew no one would hear him or care. It seemed that the warlord's men fired on planes just for the sport of it. He took one of the duffel bags slung over his shoulder and threw it to Matuma. It contained much-needed medical supplies.

Caboom! An explosion hit just behind the plane's tail section. Something fiery hot pierced Robert's left shoulder. He ignored the pain and ran faster as the plane began to pick up speed.

"There is no time, Robert. Jump on board now!" Matuma screamed.

Robert thought quickly about what was in the last bag. It held farming supplies, seeds for villagers to plant, and some picture books about good health. These he could leave on the runway. However, there were items hidden inside some of the boxes of farming supplies. Robert clutched the bag carefully. He aimed for the open door of the plane and tossed it with all his strength into Matuma's outstretched arms. He could not leave the Bibles. Those Bibles told of Jesus and of God's love for a world in darkness. Telling others about God's love was the reason Robert and his family were missionaries.

"Jump, Robert, or it will be too late!" pleaded Matuma.

Robert was terribly tired from the hard work of the last three days. His legs burned from running. Blood was soaking through his shirt from the shoulder wound. His strength was giving out fast!

Suddenly a strong hand locked around his arm. With one swift motion, it lifted him through the open door of the plane. Robert lay sprawled on the floor. The noise from the engines grew louder. The plane raced down the runway, gaining the speed it needed for takeoff.

Robert pulled himself up from the floor to one of the metal seats attached to the inside walls. Matuma closed and locked the door, then turned to look at Robert. He grabbed a metal bar above his head to steady himself as the plane lifted slowly into the air.

"I did not think you would get around to jumping for the door," he said, grinning, "so I helped you inside." Matuma was a large man and very strong. He frightened some people when they first saw him.

However, he quickly put them at ease with his gentle voice and manner.

Robert smiled back. "As always, I am grateful you are my friend," he replied. Then he gasped as a sharp pain shot through his shoulder.

Matuma frowned and knelt beside his friend. "Let me have a look." He gently tore the blood-soaked shirt away from the wound. "Ah, it appears that a piece of metal from one of the bombshells sliced through your shoulder. It does not look serious though."

Robert was deep in thought and said nothing. Matuma searched for medicine and bandages in the medical supply bag. Expertly, he began to clean and bandage the wound.

"You are thinking of the reports, aren't you, Robert?" Matuma asked.

Robert sighed and looked at his friend. "Yes, I am. The fighting and bloodshed are getting worse. The reports we have received from mission headquarters say the fighting is spreading all over Africa."

"Robert, fighting and war are not new to this land," Matuma said.

"This is different," Robert replied. "The reports say there is a pattern to the violence. It looks as though someone, or some group, is in charge of it all. Look at what we have seen the last few days. I am beginning to believe the reports."

"Do you also believe the old legend of the black jewel?" Matuma asked. He finished bandaging Robert's shoulder and sat down in the seat next to him. The plane's engines continued to roar as Robert and Matuma bounced through the air toward Nairobi, Kenya.

"I do not believe *prophecies* that are not from God," Robert answered.

"I do not either, Robert, but there are many who believe the prediction of this legend will take place."

Matuma rested his head against the side of the plane and closed his eyes. He recited the words he first heard as a small boy in his village in Kenya. "In the year of the rains and the dark sun, a great ruler will come to lead all villages. He will hold in his hand an iron rod. On the top of the rod will rest the black jewel of the sun. He is to be feared and followed."

"One government report says that the legend is being repeated in villages all across Africa," Matuma continued. "It is as though some group is spreading it, along with the violence and war."

Robert had read the report. He believed only the prophecies of the Bible. However, he also knew how an evil person could use such a story to fool people. In addition, he knew something that was not in the reports. He had heard it from a United States government worker a few weeks earlier.

"You know how the rainy season comes to most of Africa in August each year," the man had said. "Next year, in the middle of the yearly rains, there will be a total eclipse of the sun over most of Africa."

Robert shivered as he thought about the man's words. One year from now, part of the African prophecy would come true. It would be the year of the rains, and the sun would grow dark.

✽ ✽ ✽

In a mansion outside Nairobi (ny-ROW-bee), a man's black eyes blazed like lasers at another man standing before him. "Don't just stand there, you fool! Give me your report!" he said. He didn't raise his voice, but the words sent a shiver of fear down the other man's back.

"Ah, yes sir. All is going according to your plan. Professor Blake Sinclair, his wife, son, niece, and nephew landed at the Zurich airport this morning. All arrangements have been made."

The first man walked to a large window overlooking the courtyard of his mansion. He did not smile, but he was very pleased. "At long last the master plan is coming together," he thought. But that was not what pleased him the most. Certain people had made the mistake of getting in the way of his plans. Now they would pay for their mistake. The thought of revenge now brought a cruel smile to his face.

2

The Trap

There was a jolt and a high-pitched squeal of brakes. The train moved closer to the downtown Zurich (ZOOR-ik), Switzerland, train station.

Twelve-year-old Josh Hunter sat next to his 13-year-old cousin, Randal Sinclair. Josh's younger sister, Liz, sat behind them next to Mrs. Shanks. Randal's parents, Professor Blake W. Sinclair and Professor Judith F. Sinclair, were attending a scientific conference. They had hired Mrs. Shanks to show the three youngsters around Zurich.

Josh and Liz's parents were on a Work and Witness trip. They were returning to a village in Brazil where they had all been the summer before. When the Sinclairs decided to go to the conference in Zurich, they asked Josh and Liz to travel with them. "Josh and Liz will be safer in Switzerland than in the jungles of Brazil," they told Mr. and Mrs. Hunter.

"Are we almost there?" Liz asked. A large bearded man sitting in the seat across the aisle looked up from his paper and stared.

Mrs. Shanks turned and gave Liz a big smile. "Five or six more minutes," she answered in a strong English accent. Then she turned back to look out the window.

Liz wasn't sure why, but she had a strange feeling about Mrs. Shanks. Even at age 10, Liz had a spe-

11

cial gift for understanding people. Mrs. Shanks smiled a lot. She also spoke kindly to all of them. But when Liz looked into her eyes, she saw anger. It made her shiver. She wanted to say something to Josh, but she knew what he'd say. "You're just imagining things." After all, it was only a feeling. But she would keep her eye on Mrs. Shanks.

"It's hard to believe that a year ago we were hiking through the jungles of Brazil," Josh said to Randal.

"I was thinking the same thing, Joshua," Randal replied.

Since Randal's parents were both college professors, Randal often talked like one too. For example, he liked to call people by their full names. However, since he became a Christian the summer before, Randal's life had changed a great deal. He was still brilliant, but he no longer tried to impress people with how smart he was.

"Compared to being chased through the jungle by a witch doctor and gold thieves, this trip should be pretty calm," Josh chuckled.

The train gave another lurch as it pulled into the station. Liz could see people standing on walkways waiting to board other trains. Mrs. Shanks' hand was deep inside the large brown purse on her lap. She hummed to herself as she poked through the bag looking for something. "Oh, here it is," she said. She pulled out a large handkerchief and wiped her damp forehead. Liz wondered why Mrs. Shanks was hot. It was early summer and still cool in Switzerland. It was also a little chilly on the train.

As Mrs. Shanks closed her purse, Liz looked down and gasped quietly. There was a gun inside the purse!

The brakes gave a final screech as the train came to a stop.

"All right, children," Mrs. Shanks said as they stepped off the train. "Here is what we shall do this morning."

"Josh!" Liz whispered, trying to get her brother's attention.

"Be quiet, Liz, you're interrupting Mrs. Shanks."

Liz looked up. Mrs. Shanks was smiling at her, but there was no kindness in the smile.

"There are some beautiful buildings you will find interesting," Mrs. Shanks continued. Randal was interested, but Josh didn't think looking at buildings sounded like much fun. "However," added Mrs. Shanks, "first I thought you might like to take a boat ride on Lake Zurich."

Josh perked up. "A boat ride! That sounds great," he said.

"Will we still have time to tour the buildings?" Randal asked. "I truly enjoy the study of architecture."

Josh rolled his eyes.

"Oh, yes, there will be plenty of time for that after our ride," Mrs. Shanks assured him.

"Then a boat ride sounds quite enjoyable to me too," Randal said.

As they spoke, Mrs. Shanks led them out of the train station. They crossed the street to a large walkway beside a canal. Liz walked a step behind the others. She looked for a chance to tell Josh about the gun.

"How far is the lake?" Josh asked.

"Oh, no more than a 10-minute walk," Mrs. Shanks answered.

The day was beautiful. The sun shone brightly overhead. As they walked, Liz was so struck by the beauty of the Swiss city that she forgot about Mrs. Shanks for the moment. She did not see the large bearded man following them either.

"Hey, Randal, what's that?" Josh asked. He pointed to what looked like a large dollhouse in the shape of a castle. A man stood next to it turning a crank. Music drifted out from the castle.

"You mean the *hurdy-gurdy?*" Randal replied.

Josh scrunched up his face. "The what?"

"A hurdy-gurdy. Some call it an organ grinder," Randal said. He began to take on his professor tone of voice. "Such organs were probably first made here in Switzerland in the late 1700s. They spread . . ."

"Spare us the lecture, Randal," Josh said. "Just listen to the music."

Randal listened for a moment. "Ah yes. I believe the melody is from Chopin's Concerto in E minor. Lovely, isn't it?"

"Ahhhhhhhhhh!" was all Josh could say.

Liz laughed. She saw the twinkle in Randal's eye and understood. He was teasing Josh.

"There is the lake," Josh said a moment later. He pointed ahead to a large body of water.

"Yes, and I see the boats," Liz added.

There was a small park with concrete benches next to the water. Ducks and swans gathered in front of the benches hoping to be fed.

"Do we have anything to feed them?" Liz asked.

"Not at the moment, child," Mrs. Shanks answered. "Perhaps my friend with the boat will have something we can throw to them. This way, please." She turned and walked briskly down the sidewalk to the boat docks a short distance away.

Liz stood for a moment and turned in a circle. She was making a memory of all that surrounded her. She saw a blue sky, red flowers in a pot, and an old man walking a dog. Swans stretched out their long necks for food. A large man with a beard was reading a newspaper. She heard the sounds of cars and buses whizzing by.

"Come on, Liz, quit dawdling!" Josh yelled back from far ahead. Liz trotted after them, but something began to trouble her. She knew she was bothered by Mrs. Shanks; however, this was something else. *Something is not right,* she thought.

Liz caught up to the others. They passed a large assortment of sailboats, row boats, and motor boats. Finally, they came to the end of the docks. A scraggly little man popped his head up from one of the motor boats and waved. Mrs. Shanks nodded to him. "Here is my friend," she said to the children.

The boat was not new, but it was larger than most of the others tied at the docks. Mrs. Shanks walked down three stone steps to a wooden platform, then over to where the boat was tied. She motioned for the boys to follow. As she extended her hand to the scraggly man, he helped her step on board.

Something continued to bother Liz. She watched Josh and Randal jump onto the dock and run quickly to the boat. *Was it something I heard?* she thought. *No, it was something I saw. Come on, brain, think. What is it?* Suddenly she remembered. It was the large man with the beard she had just seen. He was holding a newspaper, but he had not really been reading it. He had been staring at her, just like he had done on the train.

Suddenly the engines on the motor boat roared. Liz looked up to see the scraggly man untie the ropes that held the boat and push it away from the dock. "Hey, wait a minute," she yelled. But before she could run to the boat a huge hand grabbed her arm in a viselike grip. She looked up to see the large man with the beard.

He held a small package in his hand. "Take this,"

he said gruffly, shoving it into her hand. "If you want to see those boys again, don't cry for help. There is a note inside the package and an envelope. Read the note." Then he let go of her arm and leaped onto the boat. Quickly it backed away from the dock.

Josh and Randal sat in the back of the boat, their eyes wide with fear. The gun that Liz had seen in Mrs. Shanks' purse was now in her hand. She was pointing it directly at Josh.

Liz watched in shock as the scraggly man turned the steering wheel sharply and gunned the engines. Water sprayed in all directions as the front end of the boat lifted, and it sped away.

Black Jewel of the Sun

Professor Judy Sinclair held Liz tightly as they sat on the bed in the Sinclairs' hotel room. Both of them sobbed quietly. Blake Sinclair paced back and forth. On the desk lay the package Liz had received. Beside it was the envelope, now open. Blake Sinclair clutched its contents—a one-page letter.

Liz had opened the package as the bearded man instructed. Inside was the envelope and a note addressed to her. Attached to the note had been a Swiss franc for bus fare and a train ticket. The note contained detailed instructions. It told which bus to take to the train station and which train would take her back to the Sinclairs' hotel.

The note ended by repeating the warning the bearded man had given to her. "You are being watched. Do not call for help or go to the police. If you do, you will never see your brother and cousin again."

Liz arrived at the hotel 30 minutes later. Her aunt and uncle were waiting for her in her room. At the conference, they, too, had received a written message. It stated there was an emergency and that they should return to their hotel room immediately.

"The note had my name on it, Uncle Blake," Liz said. "How did they know who I was?" She dabbed her eyes with a tissue.

Professor Sinclair stopped pacing for a moment and looked at Liz. He spoke very quietly. "This must have been planned long before we arrived."

"But why? Do they want money from us?" Liz sobbed.

Professor Sinclair looked down at the letter in his hand, then at his wife. She had read the note too.

The items you are hiding for the government of Kenya belong to me. Now I have two boys that belong to you. We shall trade. Wait for our call. DO NOT CALL THE POLICE!!!

"Go on and tell her, Blake," Mrs. Sinclair said.

Professor Sinclair pulled out a chair from the desk and sat down heavily. "Liz," he said, "Randal spent last summer with you and Josh because Judy and I were doing research in the Middle East. What we did not tell anyone was that we were only in the Middle East a few days."

"Why did you leave?" Liz asked.

"The government in Kenya, Africa, contacted us secretly. They asked us to come to Nairobi, the capital city. They needed our help in examining an unusual discovery."

Liz looked confused. "What would the government of Kenya need you to examine?"

"Not the whole government" her uncle answered. "It was the army to be exact. Something was found in a cave along the Indian Ocean. The Kenyans believed it could be a threat to their country, and they needed our help to look at it."

"What kind of help?" Liz asked.

"As you know, I study languages—especially

very old languages. Your Aunt Judy is a geologist. She studies rocks."

"I know," said Liz. "Dad said that you and Aunt Judy are the best in the world at understanding old words and old rocks."

Mr. Sinclair smiled. "It's true. We've been all over the world to study words and rocks. But we've never studied anything like this before."

Professor Sinclair grew quiet, and Liz's aunt continued the story. "They had discovered a scroll. It looked ancient. But when we tested it, we discovered it had been written no more than 40 or 50 years ago."

"That sounds old to me," Liz said.

"It may sound old to you," Mrs. Sinclair replied. "However, the scrolls your Uncle Blake studies are hundreds, even thousands of years old. The real mystery, though, was the writing on the scroll. It was in a language that has not been spoken in 1,500 years."

"But Uncle Blake said the Kenyan's needed both of you to help," Liz said. "Did they find old rocks along with the scroll?"

"All rocks are old, Elizabeth," Mrs. Sinclair corrected. "The scroll was discovered resting in a small ivory chest. Next to the scroll was a leather pouch."

Mrs. Sinclair seemed to drift in her thoughts and became quiet. She stood and walked to the window.

Liz waited patiently for a moment or two, but finally she had to ask. "So what was in the leather pouch?"

"Oh, I'm sorry, Elizabeth," Mrs. Sinclair said, still facing the window. She turned and looked at her niece. "They found a diamond. A diamond the size of a man's fist and as black as coal."

Liz's eyes grew wide as she thought about a diamond the size of a man's fist. Then she said, "I did a report in school last year about diamonds. The books told a little bit about black diamonds. And I learned that some diamonds have been found that are even bigger than a man's fist."

"That's true," Mrs. Sinclair said. "Most black diamonds are actually clear with spots of gray minerals inside. This diamond is completely black except when it is exposed to light, especially sunlight."

"What happens to it then?" Liz asked.

"The diamond changes from black to glowing red. It's like a piece of the sun itself."

"Wow!" Liz said. "But I don't understand why the government of Kenya is worried about an old scroll and a black diamond."

"It is what's written on the scroll that has them concerned," Professor Sinclair said.

"Not just concerned," Mrs. Sinclair added, "they are worried. That is why they asked us to take both items out of the country to study. They even gave us a special diplomatic bag to carry them in to prevent any questions when going through customs."

"So where are they now?" Liz asked.

Mr. and Mrs. Sinclair looked at each other. "We brought them here to Zurich," Mrs. Sinclair said. "They are in a safe deposit box at a bank just down the street."

Ring, ring! Ring, ring! Liz gasped and Mrs. Sinclair grabbed her husband's hand. They all stared at the telephone.

4

Tested Faith

"Ouch!" Randal said as his head bumped against the side of the bouncing van.

"Try to twist around so you're facing me," Josh suggested.

Their boat ride had been short. They raced across the lake to a private dock where an old delivery van awaited. "Schwartz's Tires and Auto Parts" was printed in German across the side of the van.

The man with the beard climbed in to drive, while Mrs. Shanks sat in the passenger seat. The scraggly man who had driven the boat held the boys and tied their hands. He smelled like dead fish. The end of the rope tying Josh's hands had been looped through several large tires stacked in the back of the van. The end of Randal's rope was tied to a metal shelf attached to the wall. A small window was set in the metal wall that divided the front cab from the back of the van.

At first the ride had been smooth, as they sped along paved streets. But for the last 15 minutes the ancient van had bounced along bumpy roads. Each time they hit a bump Randal banged his head.

"There, I think that's better," Randal said after twisting around to face Josh.

"How long have we been driving?" Josh whispered.

Mrs. Shanks peered through the window to check on the captives from time to time. But there was little chance she could hear the boys speak over the roar of the van's engine.

Randal looked at his watch. "About 45 minutes."

Fear and the shock of being kidnapped had kept the boys silent until now.

"What do they want with us?" Josh asked. "Do you think they're going to hold us for ransom?"

"I've been thinking about that," Randal said. "I do not believe it is money they are after. I'm sure this has been planned for a long time. They must know my parents have very little money."

Another bump sent both Randal and Josh flying. "AHH!" they each screamed, this time loud enough for Mrs. Shanks to hear. Her round face appeared at the small window. "Quiet back there or we will tape your mouths shut," she said sternly.

"Are you all right?" Josh asked Randal. He pulled himself up to sit on one of the tires.

"Yes, I think so. We're not on the main roads anymore, that's for sure," Randal said. He used his foot to drag one of the tires close enough for him to sit on. It wasn't comfortable, but it was better than the hard floor of the van.

"It looks like there's nothing we can do but sit here and be helpless," Josh said in frustration.

Randal smiled faintly. "I believe that sounds like me talking last summer, Joshua," he said.

Josh thought for a moment, then he smiled. Last summer Randal had traveled with Josh and his family on their two-week mission trip to Brazil. At first Randal had thought it was silly that the Hunters prayed so often. Anytime they were uncertain about what to do, they stopped and prayed. After seeing God answer those prayers, and after receiving Jesus as his Savior, Randal no longer thought prayer was silly.

"You're right, Randal, we *can* do something," Josh said. "My dad says that God tests our faith in Him from time to time, to make it stronger. This is one of those times."

They each bowed their heads and prayed. They prayed for protection. They prayed for Randal's parents and Liz. They prayed for wisdom to know what to do. And as they finished, Josh prayed, "Father, please change the hearts of our enemies, the people who have taken us. Watch over them and help them to do what is right."

As they finished, the van slid to a stop. The boys could hear several people speaking excitedly outside, but they did not recognize the language. There was, however, a sound they did recognize. A look of panic spread over both their faces. It was the whine of a jet airplane engine.

* * *

"What is the estimated time of their arrival?" The dark-eyed man sat behind his desk speaking on the telephone to someone in Switzerland. Though he was pleased with what he heard, his voice remained cold and hard. "Very good. The boys are unharmed? . . . Good."

The man turned his chair so that he faced the wall behind him. "You also called the Sinclairs, did you not? Have they departed? Ah, then everything is proceeding on schedule. Excellent. Follow them until they arrive here and continue to keep me informed." Without another word, he hung up.

"It is all coming together just as I planned." He spoke out loud, though no one was in the room. "Soon the legend will become truth. Soon there will be peace in Africa. Soon I will rule this land by my iron fist."

In Nairobi

Robert Simpson leaned back in his rickety chair and propped his feet up on the old metal desk. Matuma sat on the only other piece of furniture in the cramped office—a child's school desk.

Robert and his family had been missionaries in Africa for more than 25 years. They spent the first 20 years working with other missionaries in South Africa and Botswana. For the last 5 years, however, Robert had been working in parts of Africa where missionaries were not always welcome. He could do this because he worked with a group that gave food, clothes, and medical supplies to people in central Africa. Many governments welcomed groups like these. As Robert and his team helped the hungry and the sick in these countries, they also told them of God's love.

"Something is troubling you, my friend," Matuma said.

Robert had been staring off into space and hadn't noticed Matuma. He looked up, startled.

"I'm sorry, Matuma. I'm just thinking." Robert pointed to a letter that lay open on his desk. "Mission headquarters is suggesting that we pull back from our feeding projects in Sudan (sue-DAN) and Zaire (zah-EAR). They want us to wait until the fighting in those countries is under control."

"We've made great progress in those countries," Matuma said. "It would be a shame to stop."

"I agree. But that's not all they say in the letter," Robert said. He leaned forward, sat up straight, and read the last paragraph aloud to Matuma.

> "Our contacts in both Africa and the United States agree. Troops and military equipment are being secretly assembled throughout the countries of central Africa. We do not know who these troops are loyal to. However, all our sources agree they are under the direction of a single leader."

Neither man spoke for some time. Then Matuma asked, "What are you going to do, Robert?"

"I don't know," Robert replied. "But we don't have time to think about it right now. We need to get to the airport by one o'clock and pick up that medical shipment. We'll talk about this . . . no, we'll pray about this when we get back."

❊ ❊ ❊

The flight attendant walked down the aisle of the economy section of Swiss Air Flight 530. She checked to see if the passengers were prepared for landing at the Nairobi airport.

"Sir, is your seat belt fastened?" the attendant asked. She noticed the passenger in seat 23A was holding a black case tightly in his lap.

Professor Sinclair looked up. "Oh, excuse me, what did you say?"

"I asked if your seat belt is fastened?"

"Yes, it is. Thank you," he answered.

"Sir, would you like me to store your case in the overhead compartment?" the attendant asked.

"No, I need to keep it with me," the professor said.

"Then you'll have to put it under your seat. I'm sorry, but regulations do not allow any luggage . . ." Then she noticed the special emblem on the bag. She also noticed that it was handcuffed to Professor Sinclair's wrist.

"Oh, I am sorry, sir. I didn't realize this was a diplomatic pouch." The attendant quickly moved up the aisle.

Mrs. Sinclair sat next to her husband while Liz had the window seat. Normally, Liz would be excited to be looking out the window at Africa. However, she felt no excitement about this trip.

Liz shut her eyes and thought back over the past 16 hours. A man had called their room at the hotel and given her uncle instructions. They were to leave the hotel by cab, go directly to the bank, and pick up the scroll and stone. They were to put them into the diplomatic bag. Then they were to go to the Zurich airport. Their reservations had already been made for the flight to Nairobi, Kenya. Someone would meet them when they arrived.

Liz was jolted from her thoughts as the plane's wheels screeched onto the runway. She turned and looked at the fearful expressions on the faces of her aunt and uncle. How she wished she could talk to her dad and mom. But there was no way to contact them in the Brazilian jungle for another week.

It seemed to Liz that she had not stopped praying since leaving Switzerland. She wished they could all three pray together, but Uncle Blake and Aunt Judy did not do that very often. They went to church when they were back home. But God didn't seem very real in their lives the rest of the week.

"All right, here we go," Uncle Blake said as he rose from his seat. He began walking up the aisle toward the plane's door. Aunt Judy stood and motioned for Liz to walk in front of her.

"Who are we looking for, Uncle Blake?" Liz asked. They had left the plane and were walking up the narrow hallway to the main terminal.

"I don't know, Elizabeth," her uncle answered. "The man said someone would contact us when we arrived."

As they walked into the terminal, a deep bass voice spoke from behind them. "Professor Sinclair?"

Liz's aunt and uncle each turned around and said, "Yes."

Liz turned to look at the largest man she had ever seen in her life. She knew her uncle was six feet tall. This man towered over him by a foot and must have outweighed him by at least 80 pounds. The deep black skin on his shaved head glistened in the dim light of the terminal. Dark glasses covered his eyes.

"Forgive me," the man said with no kindness in his voice. "I forgot I was addressing two professors." A cold chill ran down Liz's back as the man's head turned in her direction. "I see you are all here. I trust you had a pleasant flight."

Mr. Sinclair's face flushed red with anger, but he kept his voice steady. "There was nothing pleasant about our trip. Now where are my son and nephew?"

"Follow me," the man said. He turned and walked quickly toward the front of the terminal.

A blast of sweltering heat struck them as the man led them through the front doors of the building into the morning sunshine. He walked to the back door of a black Mercedes automobile and opened it. Stepping to one side, he indicated that they should get in.

Liz's uncle hesitated for a moment as he peered inside the car. It was empty. He ducked his head and got in, scooting over to the far door to make room for his wife and Liz. The man closed the rear door, then walked around to the other side and got in behind the wheel. He looked at his passengers in the rearview mirror. "You may relax," he said. "We have an hour's drive to our destination."

6

Nowhere to Run

Robert stood at the back of his aging pickup truck. He held his hand over his eyes to shield them from the sun. He and Matuma had just picked up the medical supply shipment and were standing outside the airport freight office.

"What are you looking at, Robert?" Matuma asked. He followed his friend's gaze across the airport runway.

"Do you see that orange truck over there?" Robert said.

"Do you mean the one parked next to the private jet?" replied Matuma.

"That's the one. Do you recognize it?" Robert asked.

Matuma thought for a minute. Then he said, "Isn't that the truck that ran us off the road a few weeks ago in the mountains?"

"Yes, it is," said Robert. "I recognize the color, and I remember the smashed front bumper."

"Do you want to have a word with the driver?" Matuma asked. He remembered how angry they had been over the accident.

"No. But I am wondering why a dented orange truck is parked next to a private jet," Robert said.

At that moment the door of the plane opened and a short stairway unfolded. A woman walked quickly down the steps and over to the truck. She opened a door at the back of the truck and stepped aside.

Two boys walked out of the plane. Robert judged them to be in their early teens. They were closely followed by a large bearded man. The taller of the boys stopped for a moment. He put his hands to his eyes, as if he had not seen the sunlight for a long time. Robert gasped. The boys' hands were tied together. The large man gruffly pushed the boys from behind, causing them to stumble down the stairs. He then grabbed each of them by the arm and shoved them into the back of the truck. As he climbed in next to the driver, the truck pulled away from the plane and sped for the exit.

"Let's go," Robert cried, jumping into the pickup. He gunned the engine as Matuma hopped in next to him.

"A missionary's work is never done, is it, Robert?" Matuma asked, looking at his friend.

"We have been called to feed the hungry, care for the sick, preach good news to the poor, proclaim freedom to the prisoners, give sight to the blind, and set the *oppressed* free," Robert said, smiling. This was the answer he and Matuma always gave when Christians asked them about knowing God's will for their lives.

"So we are following the orange truck in order to set the two boys who appear to be held against their will free," Matuma said, smiling.

Robert kept his eyes on the truck but smiled as he replied, "You know how I like to obey the Scriptures exactly."

❋ ❋ ❋

Josh and Randal had spent most of their flight in a small, windowless storage area in the back of the plane. Other than their two trips to the bathroom and the times food was brought to them, the door had remained locked. They were taken from the plane with their hands tied and were shoved into the back of another truck.

"I'm beginning to feel like a piece of luggage," Josh said. He fell onto a wooden bench next to Randal.

"Silence!" Mrs. Shanks snarled, not liking Josh's humor. She sat on a bench across from them and looked hot, uncomfortable, and unhappy.

As Mrs. Shanks pulled a handkerchief from her purse and wiped her face, Josh looked at Randal. Earlier they had talked about a plan to escape. "We don't even know where we are going," Randal had said on the plane. "Where would we run?"

"Anyplace is better than being with them," Josh had replied. The boys were frightened, but they remembered the lesson they had learned last summer in the jungle. No matter how bad things were, God was always there. This gave them both courage.

Josh had suggested, "Let's use a code to let each other know when it's time to run."

"This isn't a spy game, Joshua," Randal had said at first.

"But we need a signal of some kind so we can run away at the same time," explained Josh. Finally Randal had agreed. They decided on the phrase *my stomach hurts.*

"It's perfect," Josh had said. "They will simply think one of us is sick. We will count to 10 and then run."

Now sitting in the back of the truck, Josh looked toward Randal. *Was it time to use the code?* he wondered. But Randal gave a slight shake of his head to say no. Then he glanced at Mrs. Shanks.

Josh turned to look as well. The handkerchief she had been holding was gone. In its place was her gun. She glared at them silently as the truck pulled away from the plane and left the airport.

7

The Black Castle

Heavenly Father, I'm really scared. Liz prayed silently as she looked out the window of the speeding Mercedes. *If Mom and Dad were here, we would all pray to understand what You want us to do. But there's no one here to pray with me now. Nothing surprises You, Father. You know everything that is going to happen. I trust You . . . But I'm still scared. Help me to be brave. And please protect Josh and Randal. Amen.*

Liz turned from the window and looked at her aunt and uncle. She could see the worry and fear on their faces. After her prayer, Liz felt stronger. She was still afraid, but now her attention was not on her fear but on God. She wished her aunt and uncle could do the same. She slid her hand over and squeezed her aunt's arm.

Judy Sinclair looked at her niece.

"We don't have to worry, Aunt Judy. God has a plan," Liz whispered.

Mrs. Sinclair started to say something, but her husband interrupted her.

"It looks like we've arrived."

After traveling for almost an hour, the Mercedes turned off the rutted highway. It pulled up to a large iron gate. A 12-foot-high concrete wall stretched from each side of the giant iron bars.

Four men dressed in uniforms and carrying machine guns rushed through a small door at the side of the gate. Quickly they surrounded the car. A fifth man, also in uniform and wearing dark glasses, stepped through the door behind them. He walked rapidly to the driver's door.

As the driver lowered the window, the man in the dark glasses leaned down and peered into the backseat. He then looked at the driver, who gave him a short nod. The man then made a signal with his hands. Immediately the large gates swung open.

The Mercedes pulled through the gate. It followed the paved drive as it wound through dense jungle trees. Suddenly they arrived in a clearing that was twice the size of a football field.

"Whoa!" Liz exclaimed. "It looks like a small city."

"You are correct, Elizabeth Hunter," the driver said over his shoulder. It was the first time he had spoken since leaving the airport. The way he said her name made Liz shiver.

"This is truly a small city," he continued. "There are two office buildings, a medical clinic, and three buildings where soldiers live. We also have a plant to provide electricity and water. We are completely self-sufficient."

The car followed the road as it wound around several buildings, then took a sharp turn to the right. "This is our most important building, however," the driver said. "It is the home of our future ruler."

Through the front windshield the passengers could see a huge black building ahead of them. "It's a castle," Liz said in wonder.

"Like no other in the world," the driver said.

The castle was at least five stories tall and as

wide and long as a giant airplane hangar. At first Mrs. Sinclair thought it looked black because of the shadows cast by the sun. But as they drove closer, she gave a low whistle. "Black marble," she exclaimed.

"What did you say, Aunt Judy?" Liz asked.

"The castle is built with stones of black marble," Mrs. Sinclair answered. "Black marble is fairly rare. It must have taken a fortune to buy enough for a building this size."

The Mercedes pulled into the circular drive in front of the castle and stopped underneath the covered entrance. Two uniformed men appeared and opened the back door. The driver came around and stood before Liz and her aunt and uncle.

"You will now follow me," he said. "Your host wishes to meet you, and he does not like to be kept waiting."

The Sinclairs and Liz followed the man through the huge oak doors of the castle entrance. They looked in amazement at the entry hall. It was at least three stories tall and extended back into the castle a great distance. It, too, was covered in black marble, which gave it an almost cavelike appearance. Light came from flaming torches lining both sides of the hallway. Flickering light danced eerily along the walls. The footsteps of the man and his three captives echoed loudly against the black marble.

Halfway down the hall, the man stopped and faced the wall. He reached over and touched a small button at the base of one of the torches. Suddenly a part of the wall slid to the side, revealing an elevator.

The man stepped aside and motioned for Liz and the Sinclairs to get in. He did not follow them. As suddenly as it had opened, the door slid closed and the three were alone.

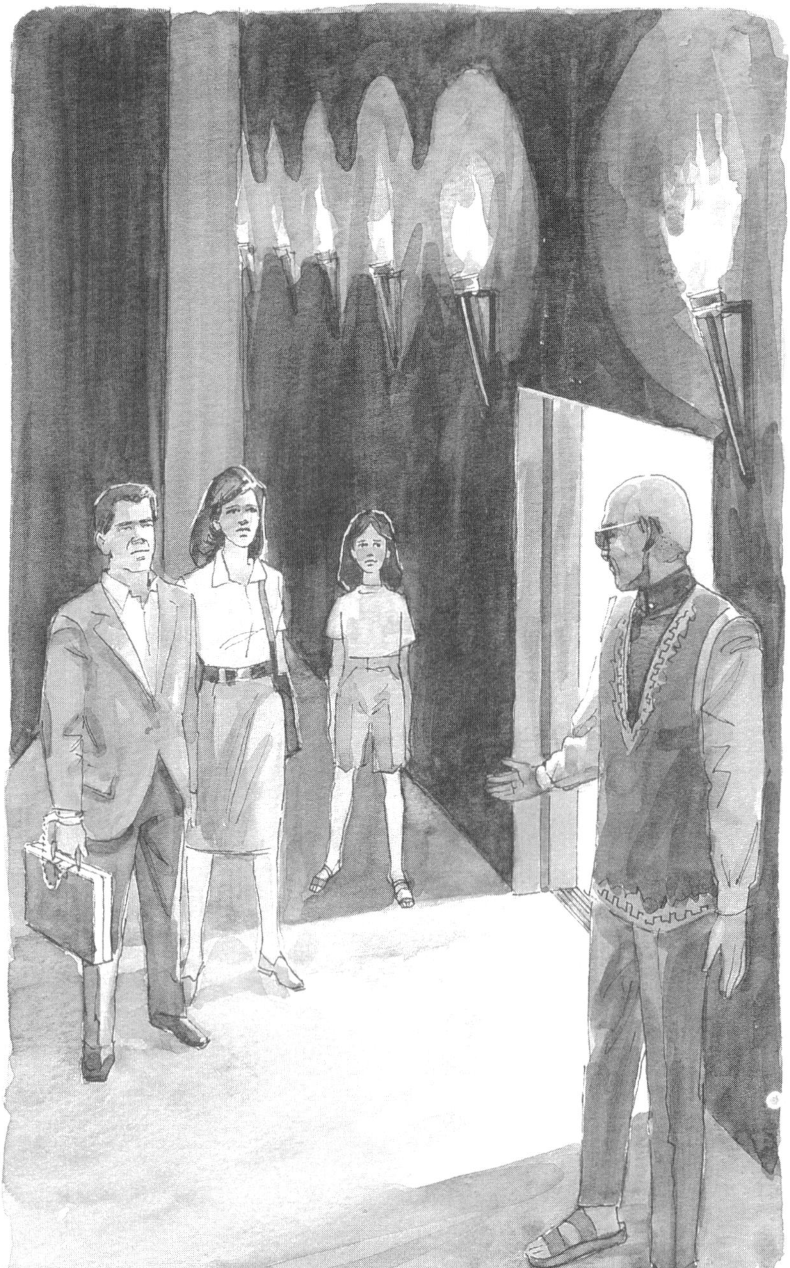

They stood quietly for a moment. Then Liz said, "I don't see any buttons to push."

Immediately the elevator began to lift. "So who needs buttons?" Liz said with a nervous laugh.

A few moments later the elevator stopped. All three stared expectantly at the door. When it finally slid back, the Sinclairs each gasped. Liz screamed.

8

He's Back

The elevator doors opened to a large room. In place of furniture, however, there were carpets and pillows on which to sit. Windows along the walls allowed bright sunlight to pour in. But even with the sunlight, the black marble that covered everything caused the room to look dark. Josh and Randal stood in the middle of the room. Their hands were tied in front of them, and large pieces of tape covered their mouths. Two military guards stood on either side of the boys, pointing their machine guns into their sides.

Professor Sinclair walked from the elevator toward the boys. His face flushed red with anger. "What kind of devil bullies young boys like this?" he yelled. His voice trembled with rage.

As Professor Sinclair came forward, the guards shoved their guns harder into the boys' sides. They each shuddered with pain. Professor Sinclair froze.

"I have been called a devil many times, Professor Sinclair," said a menacing voice from the shadows. A man stepped into view.

"I will answer your question though," the man said. "I am that kind of devil, as you call me. I will do whatever I must to see my destiny fulfilled."

✻ ✻ ✻

"Ouch," Robert yelled after hitting his head on

the roof of the bouncing truck. "Are you sure you know where you are going, Matuma?" he asked.

Matuma was now driving. A short time earlier they had pulled to the side of the road after the orange truck turned and entered the large iron gate.

"What is this place?" Robert had asked, looking at the block wall and giant gate.

"I have heard of this place," Matuma had said. "It is a military base. I have a friend who delivers food here every month or so. There is a back road that leads to another entrance for delivery vehicles."

Robert and Matuma formed a quick plan. Since Matuma knew the roads better than Robert, he would drive and get them to the back entrance. They still carried the medical supplies that they had picked up at the airport. The plan was to tell whoever was at the back gate that they were carrying medical supplies. "All military bases have doctors," Robert said.

"I've been praying since I awoke this morning. Something big is going on, Matuma, and I feel that our medical supplies are in some way a part of it."

Matuma nodded his head in agreement, then pointed ahead. "There is the gate."

"Father, protect us and guide us," Matuma prayed softly. The old pickup truck rolled to a stop in front of a large chain-link gate. A 10-foot barbed wire fence extended from either side. Two uniformed guards stepped from a small shed. One walked slowly up to the vehicle. Both held machine guns, ready to fire. Matuma handed the guard the airline receipt listing the medical supplies that had been shipped.

"We are carrying medical supplies," Matuma said. "Which way is the clinic?"

The guard looked over the receipt then looked into the back of the truck. "I was not told of any medical supplies being delivered today," he said sternly. "Wait here while I check on this." He then turned and walked quickly back to the shed.

"What do we do now, Robert?" Matuma whispered. "When he calls, the clinic will tell him there is no order."

Robert smiled and said, "Just wait and see. I don't think there will be a problem."

A moment later the guard walked back to the truck. Without a word he handed the receipt to Matuma. Then he turned and signaled to the second guard. The second guard nodded and pressed a button on the side of the shed. The gate swung open.

"The clinic is in building number 12. You will see the numbers above the doors," the first guard said. He motioned for them to proceed.

Trying to keep the look of amazement from showing on his face, Matuma put the truck in gear. He drove through the gate and followed the winding road leading into the base.

"How did you know they would let us through?" Matuma asked.

Robert chuckled. "The bigger the operation, the less people know what's going on," he explained. "I'm sure whoever the guard called thought that someone on the base ordered medical supplies. Besides, in Kenya nobody turns down a delivery of medical supplies."

✽ ✽ ✽

The Sinclairs and Liz now stood in the middle of the room. The boys and their guards were a few feet away. Liz looked at the man who now stood in front of them. He was tall and dressed completely in white. His dark skin and jet black hair made him look like

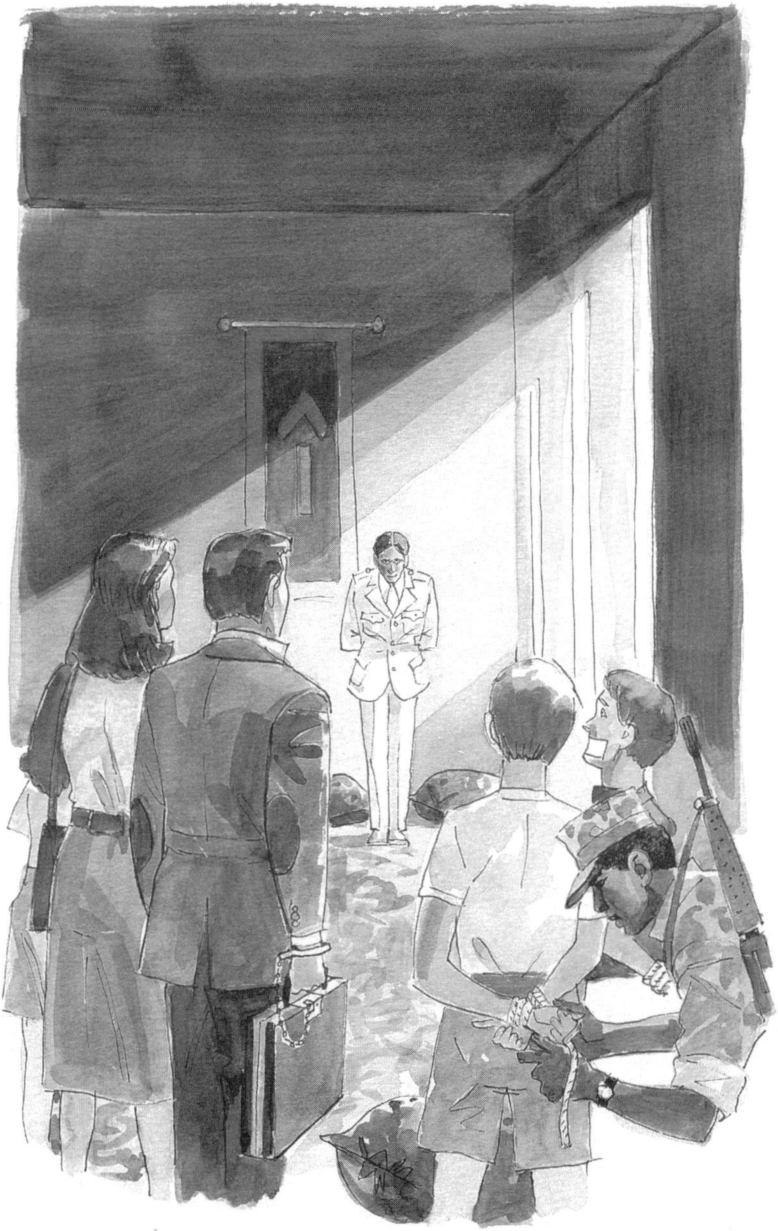

someone from the Middle East. But it was his eyes that caught Liz's attention. They were completely black. It was as though the black pupil took up the whole eye. Looking into his eyes caused her to shudder.

The man walked toward them. "Untie the boys," he said to the guards. "I believe the Sinclairs will gladly cooperate with us."

"Who are you?" Professor Sinclair asked.

"Ah, yes. We have not been officially introduced, have we?" the man said. An evil grin formed at the corners of his mouth. He took one step back and gave a slight bow.

"I am Raven Ortega, heir to the throne of Africa."

9

Inside

Raven Ortega saw the startled expression on Liz's face. "I see that you recognize my name. That is good," he said with an evil grin.

"You were in South America last summer," Liz said. "Uncle Paul wrote us that the police in Brazil were looking for a man named Raven Ortega. They said he was behind the illegal gold mining in the Amazon jungle."

"Ah, yes. Uncle Paul," Ortega said, almost spitting out the name.

The Sinclairs looked at each other in confusion. "I don't understand. How do you know him?" Professor Sinclair asked Ortega.

Raven Ortega smiled wickedly. "I know all of my enemies," he said. "I am a rich man. But completing my work takes more money than even I have. That is why I have teams of smugglers, illegal miners, and thieves all over the world. They are busy finding treasures to support my work."

Raven Ortega walked over to Randal and Josh. He put his hands on their shoulders as a friend might do. But there was no kindness in his voice as he continued to speak.

"Last summer we found the largest deposit of gold ever discovered in that South American jungle. But as we were beginning our mining, Paul, the missionary, showed up. Soon after, his do-gooder friends, the Hunters, came to visit. I hate missionaries!"

Ortega was now pacing back and forth as he spoke. "I had to flee the jungle. But before I left, I discovered the names of those who so rudely interrupted my plans. They were Dr. and Mrs. Lee Hunter, their children Joshua and Elizabeth, and their nephew Randal Sinclair." He now stood directly in front of Professor Sinclair.

"Imagine my surprise to find that other members of the family were stealing from me on the other side of the world." He then looked down at the case handcuffed to Professor Sinclair's wrist. "Remove the bag from your wrist," Raven Ortega ordered.

Professor Sinclair reached into his pocket and removed a small key. He quickly unlocked the handcuff and handed the case to Ortega.

"We have done what you asked of us," he said. "Now, take us to the airport and let us go home."

Ortega smiled wickedly. "Professor Sinclair, I am hurt. You can't be thinking of leaving so soon." He walked quickly to a large door at the side of the room. Before opening the door he turned to them. "You will all be witnesses to the greatest historical event ever to occur on the continent of Africa," he said. "Guards, take them to the clinic and lock them in an exam room." Then he disappeared through the door.

❈ ❈ ❈

Robert and Matuma had no problem finding the medical clinic. They parked and began to unload the boxes of supplies onto a pushcart in the back of the truck.

"Have you noticed the uniforms the men are wearing?" Robert whispered as they worked.

"They are not the uniforms of the Kenyan Army," Matuma answered.

"No, they're not," Robert said. "I think we've stumbled into more than just kidnapping."

"Stumbled, Robert?" Matuma asked with a smile. "Those who follow Jesus do not stumble into things. They are led."

Matuma walked ahead to open the entrance doors as Robert pushed the cart. They found themselves in a small waiting room. Other than a nurse sitting behind a desk, the room was empty.

"May I help you?" the woman said, frowning. She spoke with a strong English accent.

Robert stepped forward, "Yes, you may," he replied. "Please tell us where to deliver these medical supplies."

"You are not the men who usually deliver supplies to us," the woman said suspiciously.

"No, we're not," Robert answered truthfully.

"Let me see the paperwork for this order," the woman said coldly. She picked up the receiver of the telephone on her desk. Before she could finish dialing, however, the two swinging doors to the left of the desk burst open. A young boy ran into the waiting room, followed closely by a man in uniform.

The boy suddenly froze as he looked up and saw the woman behind the desk. The guard quickly grabbed his arm and pulled him back through the doors.

Robert and Matuma looked at each other. They both recognized the boy. He was one of the two they had seen taken from the plane. They said nothing.

The woman stood quickly and walked toward the swinging doors. She seemed to have forgotten that Robert and Matuma were there. Suddenly she said over her shoulder, "Leave the supplies and go." Then she, too, disappeared through the doors.

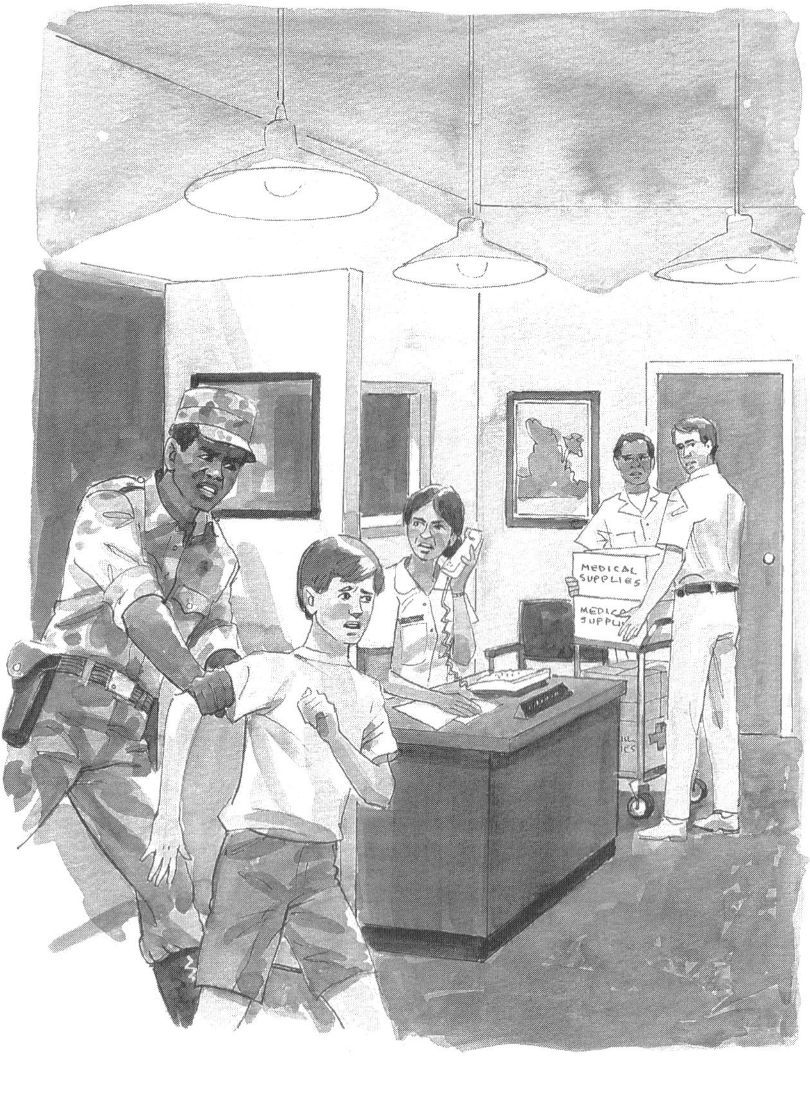
MEDICAL SUPPLIES

10

Crossed Signals

"Are you crazy, Josh! What were you thinking of?" Liz asked angrily.

Liz, Josh, Randal, and his parents were now locked in one of the clinic's small examination rooms. A wooden table and rickety chair were the only things in the room.

Randal sat on the table holding his stomach. His face was pale, and his mother sat next to him rubbing his back.

"It was our signal," Josh whispered.

"Signal?" Liz questioned.

"Randal and I decided on a signal if either of us saw a chance to run. We would count to 10 after the signal, then run as fast as we could," Josh explained.

"What was the signal?" Professor Sinclair asked.

"One of us was to say, *my stomach hurts.*" Josh looked down at his shoes a little embarrassed. "How was I to know that Randal's stomach really did hurt?"

Randal looked up. "I'm sorry, Joshua. I forgot all about the signal. I'm feeling a little better though."

Liz couldn't help herself. She began to giggle, which turned quickly into full laughter. "You mean you thought Randal was giving you the code sign to run when he told his mom his stomach hurt?" she said between laughs.

Josh and Randal began chuckling too. The Sinclairs just looked at the three young cousins.

49

"I might have gotten away if I hadn't run into Mrs. Shanks," Josh said.

At the mention of Mrs. Shanks' name the laughter stopped. She was a painful memory that everyone wanted to forget. The room was quiet for a moment.

"When I saw those guards pointing guns at you two, I wanted to scream," Liz said, breaking the silence.

"You did scream, Liz," Josh replied. "In fact, I think Mom and Dad may have heard you."

"So what do we do now?" Randal asked, looking at his parents.

Professor Sinclair looked around the room. "There are no windows," he said. "The air vent in the ceiling is not large enough to crawl through. As much as I hate to say it, we must wait for Mr. Ortega. It looks like we're in his hands."

"Excuse me, Father," Randal said, "but that is not correct." He flashed a quick smile to Josh and Liz, who each nodded their agreement. "We are in God's hands, and so is Mr. Ortega," he continued.

Professor Sinclair looked a little uncomfortable but said, "Yes, Randal, I guess you are right."

"Father, Mother, there is something I learned to do last summer that we need to stop and do now," Randal said. "We need to pray."

The three cousins reached for each other's hands. Randal reached out to take hold of his mother's hand as Liz reached for her uncle's. The Sinclairs looked at each other for a moment, then took each other's hands.

"Josh, why don't you lead us?" Randal said.

Josh began a simple prayer for God's wisdom, protection, and strength.

✷ ✷ ✷

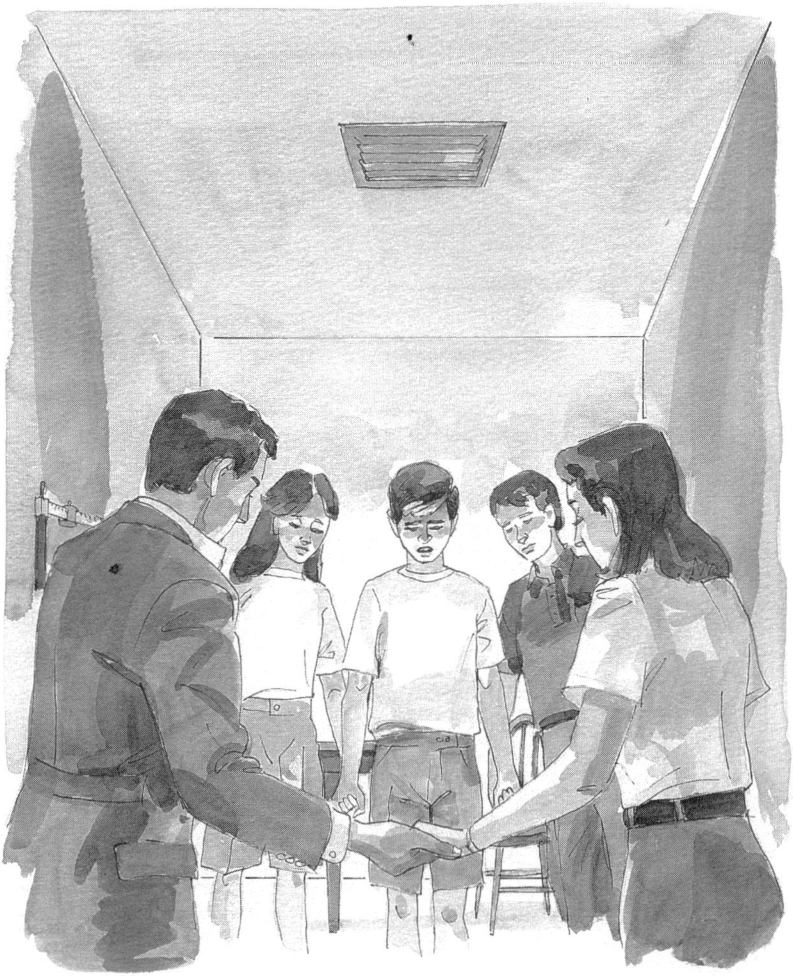

Robert and Matuma did not leave the building as the nurse had instructed. Instead, they crept toward a door on the other side of the waiting room. It was unlocked. They carefully opened it and saw a long hallway going to the back of the building. No one was in sight. Robert and Matuma ducked through the door and walked quietly down the hall.

"Do you have a plan, Robert?" Matuma asked.

"No, I thought you had a plan," Robert answered.

"I have no plan, my friend. We must wait for God to show us His," Matuma said.

"That is exactly how I have been praying. I hope He hurries up, though."

Closed rooms lined both sides of the hallway. Muffled sounds came from somewhere down the hall. Suddenly one of the doors opened a few feet ahead. Two men wearing white lab coats walked out. Robert and Matuma froze against the wall. If either of the men turned their heads slightly to the right they would see the two missionaries. Instead they walked quickly in the opposite direction.

Robert inched his way to the doorway and peered into the room. It was empty. He and Matuma stepped inside and silently closed the door. The room appeared to be a supply room. A row of lockers lined one side of the wall.

"Why did we come in here?" Matuma whispered.

Robert pointed to the doorway on the other side of the room. "I am guessing that there are two wings in this building. The boys ran through the doors on the other side of the waiting room. I hope this leads to the other wing."

Robert walked to the other door. It was unlocked. He cracked it open, then said, "I was right. It's another hallway. The boys must be in a room on this side."

Matuma placed his hand on Robert's shoulder and whispered, "I have an idea."

Robert shut the door and turned toward Matuma, who now stood by an open locker door. Matuma reached in and pulled out a white lab coat and a uniform.

"These would help us blend in, don't you think?" Matuma said, smiling. "After all, we are giving them free medical supplies. Surely they will not object to our borrowing some extra clothes."

Before Robert could answer, however, the door they had just come through suddenly opened.

11

The Explanation

Keys jangled outside the examination room. The lock turned and the door opened. A guard, pushing a cart, squeezed past the five hostages. A television sat on the cart, and a video camera and microphone sat on top of the television. The guard pushed the cart against the wall and plugged the cord into an outlet. As he turned to leave the room, he pressed the On switch.

"Maybe we get to watch a movie or something," Josh said.

"I don't believe so, Josh," Professor Sinclair said. "I think our host has something else in mind." Then turning, he spoke directly to the television. "Isn't that right, Mr. Ortega?"

A *sinister* laugh came through the speakers of the television. Then, suddenly, the face of Raven Ortega filled the screen.

"You are correct, Professor Sinclair," Ortega said. "I hope you do not mind my not coming to you in person. I have so much to do. I can see you, though, through the video camera. And you can see me on the screen. The microphone and speakers allow us to speak with each other."

"We have nothing to talk about, Ortega," Professor Sinclair said angrily.

"Maybe not. But after you witness the speech I give to my followers, you may change your mind."

Raven Ortega sat at a large desk. He leaned forward as he continued to speak. "Eighty years ago my grandfather came to Kenya with a great dream. He saw the beauty of the land and its people. But he was troubled by rivalry and fighting between the many tribes. He decided that he would work to unify the tribes and bring peace."

All five prisoners stared at the screen. Ortega's eyes seemed to grow blacker and his voice grew louder as he continued.

"My grandfather was just a dreamer though. My father watched him die at the hands of the very people he tried to help. But my father had a different plan for uniting the people. He would use fear and superstition. And his vision was not just for Kenya, but for all of Africa.

My grandfather passed great wealth to my father. He used it to travel to many African countries. As he traveled he began to spread the legend that a ruler would one day come to unite the whole continent."

"Are you speaking about the legend written on the scroll I just brought to you?" Professor Sinclair asked.

"That is correct, Professor Sinclair. You see, my father had great vision. He knew that it would take many years for the legend to be told so often that people would begin to believe it. He knew that he would be too old to be the leader of a great nation. His plan was to train someone else to be the future ruler. His son."

"What legend is he talking about?" Josh asked.

"Yes, and what was it that you delivered in that case?" asked Randal.

"Go ahead, Doctor, answer their questions," Raven Ortega said.

Professor Sinclair looked at his wife, then at the boys and Liz. "To answer your question first, Randal, inside the case was a scroll and a very large diamond. A black diamond, to be exact. The legend that he is speaking of is written on the scroll."

"So what does the scroll say?" Liz asked curiously.

Her uncle looked at the ceiling as he recalled the words.

"In the year of the rains and the dark sun, a great ruler will come to lead all villages. He will hold in his hand an iron rod, and on the top of the rod will rest the black jewel of the sun. He is to be feared and followed."

Everyone was silent for several moments. Then Ortega spoke, "My father wrote those words on that parchment paper when I was one year old. He wrote it in an ancient language, hoping people would think the scroll was very old. Then he took it and one of our family treasures, the black diamond, and hid them in a cave on our land. My father loved to read. In his studies he discovered there would be a total eclipse of the sun over Africa in August this coming year. That will also be the month of my 40th birthday."

"So your father made up the legend based on something he knew would take place in the future," Professor Sinclair said.

"That is correct. Brilliant, don't you think?" Ortega said. "His plan was to hire someone to dig up the chest a year before the eclipse. The black diamond would be brought back to us. But the scroll would be revealed to the entire country as ancient. When it was read, it would cause everyone to believe the legend."

"But your plan didn't include the scroll and diamond being discovered by strangers," Mrs. Sinclair said.

Raven Ortega's face twisted in anger. He stood. "That is correct, Mrs. Sinclair. And the plan did not include your stealing our property either," he said between clenched teeth. He walked around his desk, then faced the camera again. "But that has been corrected now. In a few minutes I will speak to my loyal followers on this compound. They will be the first to see the black jewel of the sun."

"I am curious, Mr. Ortega," Mrs. Sinclair said. "Where is your father now?"

Ortega's face filled the television screen as he spoke the words, "He is dead, dead, dead."

The screen went blank.

12

Shattered

Robert and Matuma froze as the door to the supply room swung open. A round little man wearing pants, sandals, and no shirt backed into the room. He pulled a mop and bucket behind him. He stopped and turned around, then nearly screamed in fright.

"Oh, I am sorry," he said in his language. "I thought this room would be empty."

Matuma understood his words and said, "No harm done. We were just changing. Can you come back in a few minutes?"

The little man shook his head yes and headed for the door. As he did, Matuma noticed several keys hanging from the man's belt. "Excuse me, friend," Matuma said. "We need to get into one of the rooms down the hall. Could we borrow your keys for a short while?"

The man brightened at the chance to help. "Of course," he said, untying the string that held the keys to his belt. "Use them as long as you like. Just leave them at the front desk when you are through."

Matuma took the string of keys and the man left the room smiling.

Robert put on the lab coat, and Matuma the uniform. "That was a great idea, Matuma. I was wondering what we would do if we found the room the boys are in and it was locked."

"The Lord already had that planned for us," Matuma said.

They stepped back to look at each other. "You look like a soldier, Matuma. But I don't think this lab coat makes me look like a doctor," Robert said.

"It is true you do not see many doctors wearing hiking shorts and boots," Matuma said. "But it will have to do."

They opened the door and looked both ways. The hall was empty. "OK, Matuma," Robert said. "You listen at the doors on that side and I will take this side. We will signal by whistling softly when one of us finds them."

They quietly shut the supply room door and started down the hall.

* * *

The five prisoners stared at the image of Raven Ortega on the screen, speaking to his followers.

When the screen went dark after Ortega's first conversation, the five stood in stunned silence. They tried to understand all that he had said to them. But soon the screen flashed to life again. This time Raven Ortega stood on a platform behind a large stone podium (POE-dee-um). Perhaps 200 people were gathered in a room to hear him.

Ortega spoke for a long time, but Professor Sinclair was the only one of the captives who understood the language. He translated Ortega's words as best he could. Ortega told his followers that the day for the fulfillment of the legend would come soon. A great future was in store for all of Africa.

Suddenly, Ortega stopped speaking and stared. His black eyes made contact with each of the men gathered in front of him. Then, from behind his back, he pulled out an iron scepter (SEP-ter). At the end of the scepter was the black diamond. "Behold, the black jewel of the sun, in the hands of your leader," Ortega screamed.

A murmur of excitement spread over the group. They had heard of the black jewel of the sun. But now they saw it in Ortega's hands. It made the legend that they had heard from childhood seem true. The great leader had come.

Several of the soldiers began to shout and sing. Others jumped up and down like children. Others bowed down as if to worship Ortega and the black jewel.

Ortega raised the scepter over his head. Then he brought it down hard, as if to pound the jewel on the stone podium like a gavel. But he stopped a few inches from the stone.

Mrs. Sinclair gasped as she watched the screen. "Oh, no," she said.

"What is it, Aunt Judy?" Liz asked.

"I'm afraid Mr. Ortega is in for a surprise if he hits that podium with the diamond," she answered.

They all watched as Ortega repeated the motion with the scepter a second time. Then he raised it a third time. This time he spoke in a booming voice. "Today!" His audience grew quiet. "Today marks the beginning of a new history for Kenya and all of Africa!"

As he spoke the last word, he brought his arm down hard. However, this time he hit the stone with the diamond. When it hit, the diamond shattered.

Ortega and his audience looked in stunned silence at the broken pieces.

Randal stared at the screen, then turned to his mother. "How is that possible, Mother?" he asked. "A diamond is the world's hardest substance."

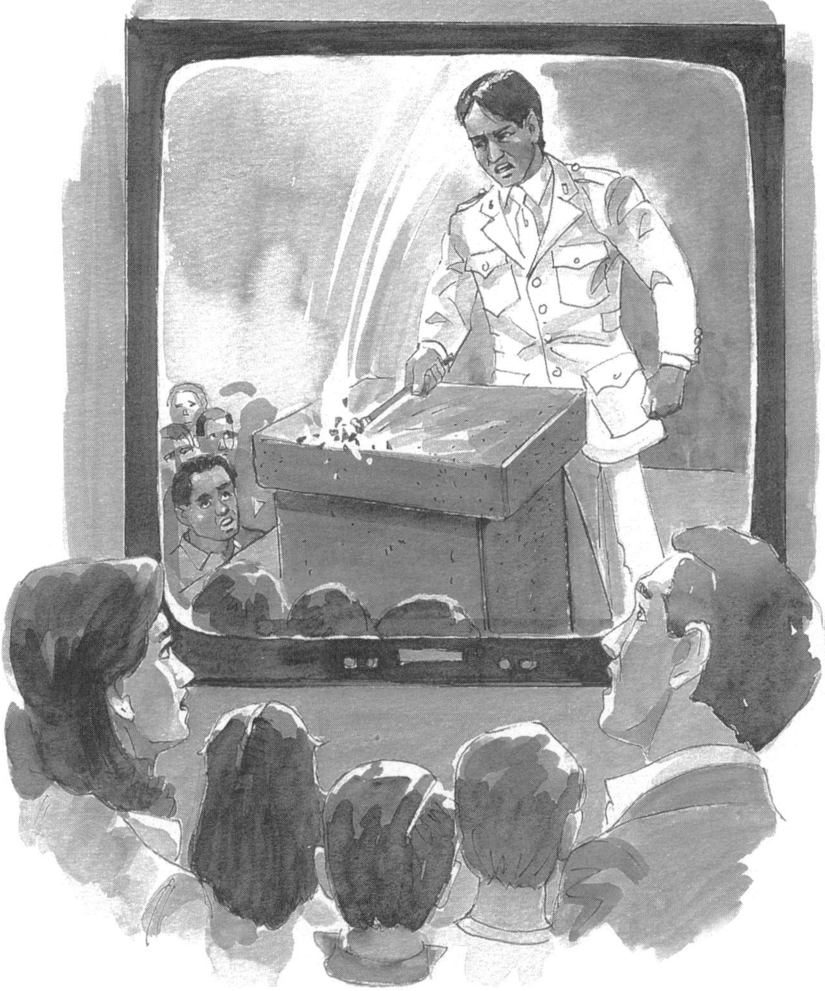

"Yes, Randal, it is," she answered. "But not this one. You remember that diamonds are made from soft black charcoal."

Randal shook his head yes.

"This diamond is black because a great deal of charcoal still remains inside it," Mrs. Sinclair answered. "It is like a diamond that is not quite finished yet. The charcoal inside keeps the stone from becoming very hard. Dropping it on the floor would not damage it. But hitting it hard against another stone . . . well, we just saw what happened."

Murmuring spread throughout the room where Ortega had been speaking. "Was this not the jewel of the legend?" some said. "Surely this cannot be our leader if he no longer has the black jewel of the sun," others said.

Raven Ortega rubbed his eyes as if waking up. "This cannot be," he murmured. "This cannot be the true stone." His voice grew louder. "We have been tricked. They did not deliver the real stone! Guards, bring the American thieves to me!" he screamed.

"Oh no, I think we're in trouble," Josh said, looking up from the screen.

"What do we do? The guards will be here from the castle in just a few minutes," Liz added.

Suddenly, there was the sound of a key turning in the door.

13

Rescued

The door to the examination room swung open as a guard stepped in. A man with a white lab coat followed behind him.

"Boy, these guys got here fast," Josh said in amazement.

Both men stopped in the doorway, looking confused. They looked at Josh and Randal, then at each other. "Are you the kidnapped boys?" the man in the lab coat asked.

"We are all prisoners here," Professor Sinclair said. "Who are you?"

"No time for introductions, I'm afraid. My name is Robert and this is Matuma. We've been sent to set you free. I'm afraid we must leave very quickly," Robert said.

"Quickly is too slow for me," Liz said, dashing for the door. "The real guards are on their way to get us right now."

Robert headed back up the hall toward the front door of the clinic. The five prisoners followed, with Matuma protectively at the rear.

The lobby was deserted. Robert peered out the front door but saw no one. The truck was still parked where they had left it. He motioned to the others to follow him outside.

"Matuma, I have an idea. You sit up front with me. The rest of you lay down in the back of the truck," Robert instructed.

No one asked questions. All five jumped into the back of the truck and laid down. Robert grabbed the end of a large piece of canvas.

"I'm going to cover you with this," Robert explained. "It may get a little warm, but don't stick your heads out until I say it's OK."

A muffled "OK" came from under the canvas. Robert reached into a side pocket of his lab coat and pulled out a red ink marker. He began to write on the canvas with large red letters. When he was finished, he put the marker back in his pocket and jumped into the truck. He saw Matuma with his hands on the dashboard praying. Robert turned the key in the ignition (ig-NISH-un). The old engine jumped to life.

As Robert backed the truck onto the road, two jeeps roared around the corner. They screeched to a stop in front of the clinic. Three soldiers jumped out and raced for the door. However, a fourth guard held up his hand for Robert to stop. He walked up to the window on Matuma's side.

"I have not seen you before," he said to Matuma suspiciously.

Robert leaned over and spoke. "This man is helping me take care of a little problem." He pointed to the back of the truck.

The guard took one step toward the back of the truck. He froze as he looked at the red letters on the canvas. He turned back to the window. "You may go." Then he turned and followed the others into the clinic.

Matuma gave Robert a strange look as the truck sped toward the back gate. "Is there something you are not telling me?"

Robert just shrugged and pointed his thumb over his shoulder. Matuma looked through the back window of the pickup. Then he smiled. The words **DANGER! DEADLY CHEMICAL SPILL** were printed in large red letters on top of the canvas.

But the smile quickly left Matuma's face as he looked back at the clinic. The soldiers were racing back to their jeeps, pointing to the pickup truck as they ran.

"It looks like our friends were not so easily fooled," Matuma said.

Robert looked in the rearview mirror. The jeeps were now on the road and gaining on them fast. Robert pressed his foot on the gas pedal. "I don't think we can outrun them to the back gate," Robert said.

As if to agree with those words, a gunshot was fired from one of the jeeps.

"Father, show us what to do next," Robert prayed as the truck bounced through a rut in the dirt road.

Another shot was fired. This one creased the roof of the truck with a loud clang.

"How far to the back gate?" Matuma asked.

Robert turned the wheel hard as they rounded a sharp corner. The truck's back tires skidded and threw dirt in the air.

"I believe it's straight ahead of us," Robert said.

Suddenly, one of the jeeps rammed them from behind. It was all Robert could do to keep the truck from going off the road.

"Will we be stopping at the gate to talk with the guards this time, Robert?" Matuma asked.

Robert couldn't help smiling at his friend's joke. He hadn't planned to crash through the gate. But with the jeeps so close, he didn't have any other choice.

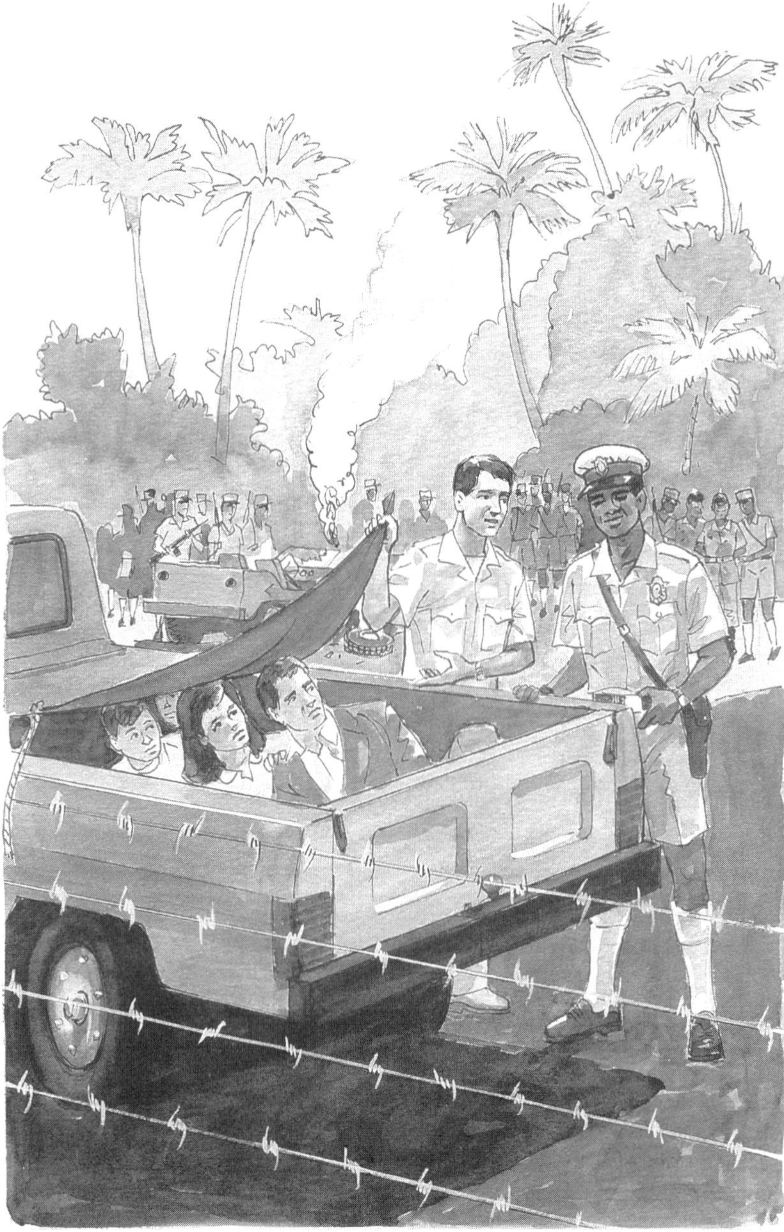

"There's the gate just . . ." But Robert never finished. His eyes got big and his mouth dropped open. He slammed his foot on the brakes and turned the truck to the side.

As the truck pulled out of the way, the driver of the jeep saw what Robert had seen. He, too, slammed on his brakes. When he did, the jeep that was following crashed into the first jeep. Both jeeps, with bumpers locked together, slid to a stop two feet from the open back gate. The men in the jeep looked wide-eyed into guns held by several hundred men from the Kenyan army and Nairobi police.

"Throw down your weapons, and step through the gate," one of the policemen commanded. The men in the jeep quickly obeyed. They were taken into custody (CUSS-tud-ee) by several soldiers of the Kenyan army.

Robert and Matuma recognized the policeman who had spoken. He was the chief of police in Nairobi. They climbed out of the truck and waved. The man waved back.

"Robert, Matuma, what a surprise to see you here," he said smiling. "You haven't by chance seen any Americans inside this base, have you?"

Robert stepped to the back of the truck and pulled back the canvas. Everyone sat up very slowly and looked around.

"Ah, the Sinclairs. How nice to see you both," the chief of police said. "And I see your son and niece and nephew are with you too. Excellent."

The man turned and walked to his own truck. At the door he turned and said, "Please excuse us. We must attend to Mr. Raven Ortega now. We will talk when I get back." With that, he and all of the men jumped into their trucks and sped into the base.

14

The Legend Dies

"I'm ready to go home now," Liz said, her mouth full of warm bread.

All five sat in a large room at police headquarters in Nairobi. Fresh bread and bowls of fruit sat on a side table. After leading his men into Ortega's base, the police chief had returned to Robert's truck. He then led them all back to headquarters. Now they were busy answering questions. A man from the Kenyan government was also present in the room.

"You see, Professor Sinclair," he said, "we have been watching Raven Ortega for some time now. We began to be suspicious when we heard rumors that his family's home was being used as a military base."

"But what caused you to raid the base today?" Professor Sinclair asked.

"One of my men saw you and your wife at the airport," the government man answered. "He reported that you carried the diplomatic case we had given you last year. He also said that you were met by one of Ortega's men. We assumed the worst and had you followed from the airport."

"Did you suspect that Ortega was behind the legend?" Mrs. Sinclair asked.

"We had our suspicions," the man replied. "But we weren't positive until you and your husband were taken to his base. A man with Ortega's wealth possessing the jewel and the scroll would have been very dangerous. We decided to raid his base immediately."

"Where is Ortega now?" Randal asked.

The government man and the police chief both shifted uncomfortably in their chairs. "I'm afraid that Raven Ortega is still at large," the chief said. "But we expect to have him in custody soon."

"He escaped again!" Josh cried. Randal and Liz shook their heads in disbelief.

"It seems that he and his sister, the woman you know as Mrs. Shanks, had an emergency escape plan," the chief continued. "But you have nothing to fear. We will have you on a plane back to the United States first thing in the morning."

Liz smiled at the thought of getting home.

Robert cleared his throat and spoke for the first time. "We have seen reports. They tell us that the wars and conflicts all over Africa may be related to each other. Do you think Raven Ortega may be part of this?"

The man from the government answered. "Officially I must say, 'No comment,' to your question. However, off the record, I believe it is a possibility. But at least we know this now. There will be no ruler appearing in a few months to claim that he is the long-awaited king of Africa."

Robert and Matuma smiled at each other. "At least not a ruler from this world," Matuma said.

The police chief spoke, "So, Robert, was it just luck that you and Matuma saw these two boys taken off the plane?"

"Oh no, sir. Luck had nothing to do with it," Robert said. "As missionaries, we've learned this. God puts us right where He wants us at just the right time."

"It is rather strange work for a missionary, is it not?" the police chief asked.

"Well it's not passing out Bibles or medical supplies, if that's what you mean," Robert answered. "But being a missionary means going where God wants you to go and doing what He wants you to do."

"I see," the chief said, getting up from his chair. The man from the government did the same. "We have no other questions at this time. Hotel rooms have been reserved for the Sinclairs. A car will take you in a short while." The two men shook hands with everyone and left the room.

The room was quiet for a long time. Then Professor Sinclair spoke to Robert and Matuma. "I don't know how to thank you two for risking your lives to save us."

"Just saying it would be fine," Matuma said, grinning.

Professor Sinclair smiled too. "OK, thank you," he said.

"I can't believe you are missionaries, though," Josh said. "I figured you were with the army or you were secret agents or something."

Everyone laughed.

"I've traveled all over the world following the Lord and telling others about Him," Robert said. "Sharing the gospel can be risky business sometimes."

"My wife and I have traveled all over the world too," Professor Sinclair said. "But never to follow the Lord. We've always been looking for more knowledge about old languages or old rocks. But we've seen the change in Randal's life since last summer. Now I'm wondering if we've spent our time learning things but never finding the truth." He looked at his wife.

"I've been thinking the same thing," Mrs. Sinclair

said. "After seeing the way the three of you prayed back there in the examination room . . ." She stopped for a moment as tears came to her eyes. "Well, I wonder what you have that we don't."

Randal looked at Josh and Liz. "I know what you need to do next," he said. He held out one hand to Liz and another to his mother. This time his parents did not hesitate. "Robert, would you start our prayer?" Randal asked.

As Robert and Matuma joined the circle, Matuma leaned over and whispered to his friend. "Now this is the kind of missionary work I really like."